Their Voices:
Their Stories

FICTION BY
BETHSAIDA ORPHAN GIRLS'
SECONDARY SCHOOL

EDITED BY JULIE WAKEMAN LINN

MKUKI NA NYOTA
DAR—ES—SALAAM

PUBLISHED BY
Mkuki na Nyota Publishers Ltd
Nyerere Road, Quality Plaza Building
P. O. Box 4246
Dar es Salaam, Tanzania
www.mkukinanyota.com
publish@mkukinanyota.com

© Bethsaida Orphan Girls' Secondary School, 2011

First Edition 2011

ISBN 978-9987-08-151-6

This edition is proudly sponsored by BancABC

Fresh Thinking. Smart Banking.

Contents

Preface

First of all, let me thank Professor Julie Wakeman-Linn for asking me to write this preface. I did not hesitate to do so because of the people who have contributed to this book: the thirteen wonderful girls. In life there are things you are asked to do, but before you do it, you have to see how you are connected to it. Their life stories, bios, and ambition have connection with mine. My own life compelled me to contribute to this edition. I was raised by a single parent, having lost my father at the age of 13, so it was very hard to refuse to write a preface to help these girls who are also struggling to gain a place in university and work to achieve what I have achieved. Their lives mirror mine; their happiness and ambition gives all of us hope and purpose for living. They are the future of Tanzania.

Let me congratulate all those who thought of this project and helped with it. I also want to congratulate the girls for taking their time to write these stories. I have read all the stories and they are wonderful. These stories, have humor, love and friendship. From the friendship of Comfort and Charity to the lessons of Chief Seketo, these tales reflect real African life stories. The variety of styles and topics make for a very lively collection. In their fiction, they mirror the joy and pain of life in Tanzania.

It is my hope that all young people who read these stories will be inspired. I pray to God that these girls' dreams become true and they achieve success so they can become lawyers, judges, bankers, accountants and even writers.

Dr. Marcellina Chijoriga
Dean, University of Dar es Salaam Business School

Editor's Note

Their Voices: Their Stories, Fiction by the Bethsaida Orphan Girls' Secondary School.

UNICEF estimates that Tanzania has over three million orphans. The Bethsaida Orphan Girls Secondary School seeks to help the "most vulnerable of Tanzania's children, the country's adolescent female AIDS orphans," according to their website, www.oloforphans.org.

Founded by Mrs. Anna Machary in 2005 under the auspices of the non-governmental organization, the Olof Palme Orphans Education Center, the school currently enrolls over 130 orphan girls from all over the country, providing them with free housing, meals, psychological support and a quality secondary education. It also provides scholarships to its Form IV graduates to complete secondary schooling or vocational training in other institutions. Bethsaida offers a rigorous preparation for the national Form IV exams which qualify students to enter Forms V and VI to prepare for A-Levels and college admission. Government scholarships are available for orphans who qualify for university, but the gap has been to complete secondary school. There are not enough secondary school places in the country and orphans are further excluded by the costs involved. Bethsaida aims to fill this gap for its students. It has no permanent funding partnerships and relies on charitable donations from individuals, churches and organizations.

In this situation, the girls receive the best possible education in the national basic curriculum; I talked with their core teachers, a hard-working dedicated group, but there has been no money for an arts or humanities curriculum. Then I entered the picture: a professor of English and creative writing on leave with time on my hands. I met Beverly Brar and I was recruited to volunteer to teach writing in my second month in Tanzania. I wanted to offer them something they didn't have any access to—so I developed a creative writing workshop curriculum especially for them.

Although I have taught college English for over twenty years, I had never taught high school students. I prepared but was apprehensive: would they listen at all, how was their English, and finally would they even want to write fiction? From my first moment in the classroom, when they stood as one and chanted, "Welcome, Professor" I knew this was going to be a unique experience. Unlike my American and international students, these girls listened to every word I spoke but they were too shy to answer any questions. I cajoled them to volunteer their ideas. My outgoing and interactive style and their quiet classroom were not a perfect fit at first. By week two, I teased them, calling them my "quiet doves". The metaphor gave them confidence, or they got used to me, and they started to flock around me after class and giggle, chirping and cooing. The girls eagerly drafted their fiction and I was amazed. The very first story came to life through magic realism. Another is a fable retold to make us laugh. One is even an emotionally intense recreation of the Civil Rights Movement in the U.S. The girls created stories of friendship and the power of self-help through hard work and education. Most of their stories end happily, often with a proverb or a bit of wisdom. Many use a deus ex machina in the form of a mysterious kind man who saves the orphan children. Some stories, like "A Street Girl," do not end happily. The student writer resisted a positive outcome even though the plot pointed to it; I believe she was too aware of the real prospect of poverty.

The girls went through a multiple stage writing process of drafting, sharing, revising and drafting. Over three months, they became writers; by the end, I was thrilled that my quiet doves would now defend their ideas, their language, and their style.

You will enjoy the humor and be horrified at the abuse experienced by the characters. The stories have a special quality; the syntax and sound of Kiswahili underlie the English words. There is a rhythm, almost a music, in their writing that we, my editorial team, have carefully preserved. Even the use of past or present progressive verbs echoes the lifestyle and the politeness of the Tanzanians that I have met and worked with. Here are a couple of tips to help you enjoy the stories. A "bajaji" is a three-wheeled mini-taxi. "Lived in a poor condition" is the girls' euphemism for stark poverty with daily hunger and certainly no money for shoes, school fees, or books. They couldn't describe a dead body, even though it is apparent that they have seen them in their young lives.

Before coming to Tanzania I edited the *Potomac Review*, a literary magazine which has received national recognition and an international readership; unlike the contents of the *Potomac Review* the girls' stories are not literary fiction; they are more real in their naiveté and simplicity. Their stories are about families lost through disease or car crashes, about relatives who abuse or neglect, but they are also stories of friendship and how education is the golden ticket desired by the characters more than anything. I was not teaching memoir or autobiography in the workshops; these are imagined stories although I know the girls have drawn on their experiences or events from their best friends' lives.

A number of individuals and organizations deserve my heartfelt thanks. Banc ABC, our own angel patron, is recognized on its own page. Thank you again, Mr. Bornface Nyoni and the board of Banc ABC–Tanzania. Working with the editorial team at Mkuki na Nyota has been a dream come true. Thanks to my employer, Montgomery College for this sabbatical leave and always a special thanks to Dean Carolyn Terry, a great boss and a wonderful friend, for encouragement and understanding. Beverly Brar is practically Mama Bethsaida, certainly its special friend, and I am so glad to have been encouraged by her to teach the girls. Gabriella Felix and Christine Mbori, Headmistress and Bursar of the school, thank you for allowing me land in the middle of the curriculum, and for welcoming me every time I arrived. To Mr. Uiso, history teacher, and Mr. Kilawe, geography teacher, thanks for sharing your classrooms with me. Lucas Ziemas' photos of the school and girls adorn this edition. Erika Koss read from afar to help me shape this volume; Lucy Duddy was a wonderful on-site reader and also cheerleader for this project. Mr. Machary, who carries on his wife's legacy of Olof Palme Orphans Education Center, deserves praise and support for his continuing efforts to fulfill the mission of the school. Dr. Marcellina Chijoriga, Dean, University of Dar es Salaam Business School, a thank you for contributing your words to this edition. I know it will inspire these girls to achieve their dreams of attending the

University of Dar es Salaam. This publication has two purposes. It is a fundraiser for the school, and thanks to our sponsors the purchase price will go to Bethsaida and to future editions. Thank you for your support through buying this copy. Above all, the purpose is to give the girls a voice. Lucy Duddy observed, this book will "make the girls realize they count and that what they have to say (about anything) is important to someone." Like me and you. Enjoy.

The Magika Tree

Anna Joseph

Once upon a time there was a village called Makifu in Uganda. Many people in Makifu were farmers. There was one boy called Madunde who was usually smart and confident and obedient. He was living with his uncle called Semiono and his aunt called Nyakomba who were also farmers.

There was a garden with many trees that were big and tall behind their house. In the garden there were good fruit trees like oranges, apples, bananas, coconuts and avocadoes. There was a big shining tree called Magika Tree. It had green leaves and smelled like roses. It also changed in different shapes like from short to tall or big to small. Sometimes the leaves changed in color like green to black, white to red. All those adaptations made people in the village wonder. It was producing fruits which were also changing from blue to white. People named those fruits as Makundedunde.

Also the Magika Tree produced water to help the people living in that village. People wondered and asked themselves, "where is the water coming from?" They were asking themselves because they knew nothing about the Magika Tree, except Mr. and Mrs. Semiono, who knew everything about the Magika Tree. The water was coming from the roots of the tree.

Mr. Semiono told Madunde he must water the garden always. Madunde did everything which his uncle told him and he respected him, but Madunde liked to play in the garden where he climbed the different trees and also ate different fruits. He was every day climbing different trees in the garden except the Magika Tree because he was afraid of its different adaptations like changing in color and shapes. But he was every day enjoying the good smell of its fruits.

One day as he finished watering the garden he looked at the Magika Tree, which was beautiful and smelling like roses. As usual the tree was changing in color and shape. It had good flowers which were beautiful yellow and wonderful white which attracted him.

When Mr. and Mrs. Semiono went to their farm, Madunde remained at home. Madunde went to water the garden and he saw fruits and leaves of that tree changing in color, leaves changing to white while the fruits changed to red. He wondered at what he saw. He finished watering the garden and he went back to the house.

Another day Madunde went to the garden and there he saw three villagers who went to fetch firewood. The villagers cut down the branches of the Magika Tree for firewood. At that moment, another five villagers again came and cut other branches of the Magika Tree. Magika Tree turned to black. When his uncle came back home, Madunde told him what had happened. Uncle Semiono told Madunde "when you see them, tell them to stop that habit."

The second day Madunde went to check the vegetables in the garden and saw many of the leaves, now brown, were on the ground and some few fruits from Magika Tree were there. Madunde collected those fruits and leaves and hid them in the dumping place outside the garden.

In the dry season, Madunde saw ten villagers going to fetch water in the garden. Because everyone wanted to get more water, they decided to hurt the roots in order that everyone could get it faster. The water was white like a spring because it was so clean. Madunde saw them hacking the roots and went to tell his uncle what was happening.

The next morning Uncle Semiono called the meeting and announced to the villagers what they did was not good. He explained to them that Magika Tree is the king of that village. So they should respect the king. Also he explained the rules of the Magika Tree except for one—Magika Tree can talk. No one is supposed to climb Magika Tree. The second rule was no one was supposed to take any fruit without permission. Third no one was allowed to cut out the roots because there is not any kind of tree which produced water except Magika Tree. The villagers heard what uncle Semiono was talking about. When the meeting finished, everyone went home.

But that was not the end for them to stop what they were doing. They were again and again cutting the tree and hurting the roots. Uncle Semiono told them every day to stop doing what they were doing because it was bad. The tree was angry for what Makifu villagers were doing to it.

Three days later when his uncle and aunt were at their farm, Madunde wanted to climb the trees. He went to the garden and started climbing the Magika tree. He had a memory about what his uncle told him about the Magika Tree, but he wanted to see what would happen. So as he was climbing the tree, he smelled a bad smell like a perfume which was too sweet, but he was still climbing the tree until the top. He found a good branch. Then he sat and picked a fruit which was near to him. Then he started eating.

As he was eating, the tree started swaying slowly which made Madunde feel good and he was saying to himself, "I didn't know this tree was so good. I feel like sleeping on this tree." He said as he started lying on it. The tree felt even more angry and increased the shaking. It shook and shook, but Madunde was not afraid. And he said again to himself. "This tree can not make me climb other trees or stop me from climbing on it and that is what I'm going to do. I will be climbing it every day," he said to himself as he was swinging on one of the tree's top branches.

The tree felt more angry and soon it started moving. It lifted up its roots and it took a step toward the village. The tree thought 'this boy might not know who I am. Let me show him who I am. Then he will not be climbing on me every day.' Suddenly Madunde was chained by the tree's branches. He started trembling. He was now afraid of the tree and he wanted to climb down, but he couldn't.

And suddenly the tree started talking, "Who are you to climb on me?"

Madunde was quiet because he did not know where the voice was coming from.

"I'm asking you—who are you to climb on me?" the tree shouted. The noise came from below the roots.

Madunde was trembling with a lot of tears. Madunde was usually smart and confident but he was afraid to answer the tree out loud.

As the tree was talking to Madunde, the whole village was arriving. People were afraid as they heard a voice from the Magika Tree and they all went to listen to what was going on. Soon they were all under the Magika Tree, watching.

The Magika Tree started beating Madunde, saying "Maybe you don't understand me." So Madunde was slashed by the tree all over his body. He was very afraid and he said, "I'm – sorry."

"I'm not asking you to tell me if you are sorry or not," shouted the tree. "I am asking you, who are you to be allowed to climb on me?"

"I'm nothing," he said, murmuring.

"Then who allowed you to climb and eat my fruit," Magika Tree yelled.

"Nobody but I'm sorry. Forgive me. I will not repeat this again," Madunde said, pleading.

"No, I'm not going to forgive you. I am going to teach you a lesson."

Down below the tree, people were afraid and they all knelt to the tree and shouted, "Don't show him a lesson. Don't, please! We are very sorry."

"Who told you to take the fruit?" The tree had become dark blue. Madunde answered, "No body !"

The tree screamed at Madunde loudly, "Do you know me!"

Madunde lied, "I don't know you."

Suddenly the garden was full of people who listened to the tree and felt mercy on Madunde but they were also afraid for their lives.

The tree said, "You people do not have minds. I helped you with many things, but now you are doing bad things to me. You are cutting down my branches for firewood, my roots for medicine and my stem for timber by using bad methods. Remember that if you exploit me more than what I can produce, I may kill all the human beings because I am the one who provides fresh air, food, and gathers the rain for your water."

People pleaded, saying to the Magika Tree, "forgive us, our king."

The tree said, "No matter. You become sorry or not, but I'm not going to forgive him. And I'm going to kill him first. Then you will follow."

Mr. and Mrs. Semiono were coming from the farm when they heard a big voice. They ran to get back home faster. When they reached home, they saw all the villagers were in their garden. And Mr. Semiono saw Madunde in the tree. He decided to go inside his house and take out a knife. He came out and put down that knife by the roots of Magika Tree. Then he started to talk with Magika Tree. "Please my king, forgive my lovely Madunde."

But the tree was so angry. Two minutes passed in Makifu village and no one talked, only listening to what would happen.

"I can not forgive him," the Tree finally replied.

Uncle asked, "Why not?"

Tree answered, "because I' ve told you about me. So why have you done this to me ?"

Uncle cried, "Please ! Magika Tree. Forgive him. It is my fault. I didn't tell him all about you, about the air, the food, the water and your ability to talk and think. My king tree, please forgive him".

But the tree shouted, "I am a king, but why you will not respect me, so now I am going to kill you all in this village."

People, again crying loudly, said to the Magika Tree. "Forgive us. We will not repeat this again, our king."

Suddenly the Magika Tree said, "How can I forgive you people?"

Uncle knelt down, under the Tree's raised roots. Then he replied, "We will give you 1000 of cows and 500 goats and 100 of pigs, our King."

All the villages said, "Yes, Yes, Our king."

The tree again said, "I forgive you and this boy, but I will punish you. I want you to respect me."

When all was finished, Madunde came back down and everyone went back to their houses and their ordinary lives.

After that day the Magika Tree produced blood instead of water and poison fruits instead of good fruits and also they were bad smelling like decaying oranges. People were vomiting and dying because of disease and the lack of water.

After three days, Madunde reminded his uncle the bet he made with Magika Tree. Madunde's uncle agreed and he reminded the villagers all the things they promised the Magika Tree. In the end the villagers found cows, pigs and goats and brought them to the Magika Tree. There after they celebrated together and Magika Tree produced water as the previous days. Furthermore Madunde become a good boy and he always listened to what his uncle and aunt told him. All those problems stopped and all the villagers lived in happiness.

The Hare, The Hyena and The Dog

Dorice Peter

A long time ago the hare, Frank, the hyena, Junior, and the dog, Brad, used to live as great friends even though other animals would always shudder with amazement how these animals could be so friendly and yet so different from each other.

One day, Junior was invited to a party by his father- in law. Like a good friend, he decided to ask his friends to accompany him to his father-in-law's party for a feast. The friends on their part did not disappoint him and they agreed to offer company.

Junior and his friends were given a reception of the highest degree. When the friends were eating, Junior and his father-in-law were dancing.

When darkness came and it was already nighttime, the hyena, Junior, and his friends were shown where to sleep. This was in the same room where sheep and goats were kept. But greedy Junior could not be trusted. In the thick of night all the animals were deeply asleep except Junior . Greedy Junior could not control his hunger because he was not eating when his friends were eating —he was busy dancing. He kept yawning and swallowing the saliva of a glutton and glancing at the sheep near him. He stealthily walked to one corner of the room and grabbed a sheep by its throat so as not make noise and awaken Frank and Brad.

Very quickly Junior strangled and ate the ram. Then he carefully smeared blood on the lips of Frank and Brad and then went to sleep as if nothing had happened.

But Junior's trick did not quite work. His friends licked their lips while they still asleep and they became as clean as they had been before. When Junior's father in- law went to check his flock, he discovered that one ram was missing. He at once asked his guests to explain who was responsible for the ungrateful act. Nobody answered, and perhaps the matter would have ended there, but the hare Frank through it was a chance for him to track down the thief so he called Junior's father -in -law and whispered for a little while.

Junior's father-in – law rushed out, and no sooner than he had left, he reappeared. He returned brandishing a panga in his hand and shouting viciously, "I have discovered the thief who killed my ram and I am going to teach him reason. I will slash and crush him like wheat for flour."

Junior was already trembling with fear and trying hard not to show it. He was panic-stricken. Suddenly Brad, who suspected he might be guilty himself, dashed out and ran as fast as his legs could carry him. Brad's escape made the father-in-law wrongly blame him for the offence. This is why the dog and the hare do not see eye to eye. Greedy, sneaky Junior left laughing because he was feeling good that he got away with killing the ram.

The Trial

Cecilia Mwanayongo

The case had started in the outlying village of Bodibeng, but it was of such rowdiness that it was brought to the central village, and of such importance that the whole village of Bodibeng turned up to witness the trial.

A certain old woman of the village named Mam-Boloi, was charged with allegedly practicing witchcraft and so certain was the village of her guilt that they frequently forgot themselves, and burst out into loud chatter. They had to be brought to order by the president of the court with threats of fines.

Evidence was presented to show that Mam-Boloi had always lived a secret and mysterious life apart from the other villagers. She had caused the deaths of many children and even brought strangers into the village. The doctor came and, while his evidence was brief and to the point, he fidgeted throughout his testimony. Yes, it was true, he said, there had been a surprising number of children's deaths in the village of Bodibeng, and death in each case had been due to pneumonia. And also a young woman had died of a septic womb due to having an abortion performed with a hooked and unsterilized instrument.

Mam-Boloi defended herself, saying, "I am a good mom. I cannot do anything bad to children because I love them from my heart. And I did not engage in any abortion."

All that was left now was for Chief Seketo to pass judgment on the case.

"People of Bodibeng," he said, "it seems to me you are all suffering from derangement of the brain." He paused long enough to allow the village to look at each other uneasily. "Your children die of pneumonia," he thundered "and to shield yourselves from blame, you accuse a poor old woman of having bewitched them into death. Not only that, you falsely accuse her of a most serious crime which carries the death sentence. How long have you planned the death of a poor old woman, deranged people of Bodibeng? How long have you caused her to live in utter misery, suspicion and fear? I say -can dogs bark forever? Oh no, people of Bodibeng today you will make payment for the legs of the old mother who has fled before your barking. The fault is all with you and because of this, I fine each household of Bodibeng one beast. From the money that arises out of the sale of these beasts, each household is to purchase warm clothing for the children so that they may no longer die of pneumonia."

He turned and looked at the old woman, changing his expression to one of kindness.

"As for you, Mother," he said "I cannot allow you to go live once more among the people of Bodibeng. Who knows what evil they will now plot against you? I have a large house and you are welcome to the protection it offers. Besides I suffer from ailments for which I am always given a penicillin injection at the hospital. Now I am tired of these injections and perhaps your good herbs may cure me." He stood up, signifying the end of the case.

So after that the chief left and the old woman went to live with him in his large house peacefully and had a lovely life. Mam-Boloi cured the chief and after a few days he was feeling better. She also helped to cure many villagers who were suffering from different diseases. With the chief, these villagers advised the people of Bodibeng village to change their habits and to stop accusing people of witchcraft. Many people understood that she was a very nice and helpful woman and they also started to love her and finally she became very famous. Mam-Boloi taught the chief how to use the herbs for curing different diseases including pneumonia and so the chief also cured people.

The people in the village loved their chief more because of the old woman and they changed and improved the village of Bodibeng as years passed. One day the old woman woke up early in the morning. She was feeling cold and all her body was trembling. She couldn't talk or say anything. After a few minutes, she died. At that time the chief was still asleep and when he woke up, he was very surprised to find Mam-Boloi had died. He made a lot of noise as he shouted, "mamaaa, mamaaaaa," but Mam-Boloi's body didn't respond to him.

Many people in village came running, wondering what had happened at the chief's house .When they realized that the old woman had passed away, they were all very sad and they were thinking about all the diseases that Mam-Boloi had cured in the many people in the villages. They also thought about the changes which she brought about but it was too late because she had already died.

They buried her and held a ceremony for three days. In the years after, the chief knew the herbs the old woman had used to cure people, so he continued curing the villagers and they all stayed well, remembering the old woman.

A Loving Relationship

Jackline Njawa

There was a girl who was called Caren and she lived in Arusha. Both of Caren's parents died five years ago when she was fifteen years old because of an aeroplane accident. Her Aunt Rose took care of her and decided to stay with Caren after Caren finished her studies in 2008 at university. Rose and Caren lived together, and had a loving relationship.

When Caren was finishing her studies, she had a boyfriend. His name was Anton. They loved each other. Their plan was to get married in the future. They enjoyed activities together very much like swimming and eating dinner together with Anton's family. But after a year had passed, Caren found that Anton had another woman who was called Helen. One day Caren went shopping and she saw Anton holding Helen's hand. Caren was upset and told her aunt what she saw. Her aunt said, "I am glad. Anton is not good."

After that Caren decided to breakup their relationship. Caren was lucky because later on Anton got HIV/AIDS. At first Anton did not know, but after one year Helen recognized that she had HIV/AIDS. Anton also started to suffer from HIV/AIDS.

Caren got a new boyfriend who was called James, who was an educated person. He was working in a big international organization called World Health Organization. After being in a relationship, he decided to marry Caren. Caren got pregnant and then she gave birth to twins. The children were called Janeth and Jonathan.

Unfortunately Anton died from HIV/AIDS with his girlfriend, Helen. They left one child called Alice. Caren's life now was happier rather than the first time with Anton. After the death of Alice's parents, Aunt Rose suggested that Caren and James adopt Alice. But Caren's husband refused because Alice was not their daughter. Caren and

Rose convinced James to agree to adopt her because they knew that if Alice lived with her relatives, they might try to take her inheritance and she might be forced to live in poverty. They brought her to their house and to school as well.

James was transferred to England with his family for a job and his children continued with school in England. Caren and James grew successful as they grew old and they returned to Tanzania. After years passed Janeth, Jonathan and Alice finished their studies. Jonathan started campaigning for people to choose him because he wanted to become a president. His dream of becoming a president came true. And now Jonathan became the President of Tanzania while his sister Janeth became a doctor, and Alice became a professor. They lived happily together.

No sweet without Pain

Dorice Kessy

Once upon a time there was a girl named Karen. When she was six years old her parents died during the war that happened in 1990. When Karen was eight, she and her aunt moved to Dar-es-Salaam where they stayed in Manzese. Karen's aunt was HIV positive, due to her poor life when she could not afford her basic needs and soon she died too. Karen was now nine years old and left alone with nobody to care for her.

Life in Manzese was so tough. She did not know if she would eat or drink each day. She was always begging for food. Some people were trying to help her but some evil boys were trying to rape her. She usually cried when she thought of all the terrible things that happened in her life.

One day when Karen was begging for food, a wise man who was in his car saw her. The man gave her some money so she could get something to eat. But when he was giving her some money, one boy who was a thief, saw her and took all the money she had been given. The wise man felt so sorry for her. The man was so religious and kind, so he decided to help Karen.

The man took Karen to the hospital as she was sick and she got medication. When Karen recovered, the man asked Karen about her life and if she had ever gone to school. She told him that she never gone to school yet and she wanted so badly to go. He compared her to his own daughter because Karen had the same height and face like his own daughter. So he took responsibility for her.

The man took Karen to his home and he asked his wife to give her food. The man was called Mr. Michael, who was the headmaster in a school called Mpigi Magoe Primary School. He had a good house, luxurious cars, and he was also owned a secondary school called Mwakanga girl's secondary school.

Karen studied at Mpigi Primary School where she finished her primary education. She did so well on her exams that she was selected to join at a secondary school called Mivinjeni Girl's Secondary School, where she studied from form one to six. After that, she also did well and she was selected to enroll at the University of Dar-Es-Salaam. Karen's dream was to be a banker. Due to her efforts of studying very hard, she became a banker at CRDB Bank. After university she became a manager of the Bank.

Now Karen has a good life. She helps every one who needs help. She also helps her adopted father, Mr. Michael, by helping to take care of his mother, who is sick. In 2009 she met a boyfriend called Brad and in 2011, they got married. They had a baby girl who they named Diana. Karen taught her daughter good behavior and how to help people who need help. Since then Karen, her husband Brad, and their daughter, Diana, have lived happily forever.

The Day to Remember

Chiku Shabani

It was in 1996 when we went to visit our relatives in Uganda with my family. We were in the car, and suddenly we saw a big car coming at high speed. We thought the driver of that car was a drunk, but we were on a narrow road, so it was difficult to find another way to pass. Immediately our car smashed into the big car.

Many people who were in our car died and my parents died. My young sisters Ashura and Aisha were injured; Ashura broke her leg and Aisha broke her left hand. I was very confused thinking what to do to help the lives of my young sisters. In a few minutes the ambulance came to take the injured ones and my young sisters were taken to the hospital. When I got to the hospital, Ashura and Aisha asked me about our parents which was a very difficult question to answer. I decided to ask the assistants to help with the money to buy food and treatment because I thought, "people would like to help me."

I went to our relatives who were there at the hospital, Aunt Hadija and Uncle Masudi, but they refused to help us. One patient shared food with my young sisters, but her relatives found out and stopped her. I was crying without knowing what to do. Also my young sisters didn't get treatment because all the doctors asked me for the money. I explained to them that I didn't have money. Then they said "it is impossible to treat your young sisters without paying anything. You may treat them yourself." I was very confused. I sat down on the floor and continued to cry.

Soon after, I saw one doctor called Magasha, who had white hair, walking slowly down the hall. I followed him and asked again for a helper, but he asked "which kind of helper you need?" Because I was confused, I said "help with treatment". He asked again for whom, and

I said for my young sisters injured in the accident. "Yes, don't worry. I will help you, but where are your parents?"

I replied "My parents died in the accident." Dr. Magasha then helped to treat my young sisters.

We heard the announcement that all people who had relatives who died in the accident should come to the hospital and take the corpses. When we went to take the corpses of our parents, we found them in a very horrible state because they were badly damaged. We went again to ask those relatives to help us to carry their bodies and they said, "We don't have money to carry them. If you give us money, it is possible. Then you can call us to get them and then we will go with you, okay?"

But even then, Aunt Aziza said, "Go. We don't want to see you again."

When our aunt was talking rudely to us about how they don't want to see us anymore, Dr. Magasha, the one who treated my young sisters, appeared and took pity on us.

Dr. Magasha helped us to carry our parents' corpses in his car. We went with him to his home. There we met with his family. He had three daughters known as Amina, Mwajabu and Sabrina. All of them were studying at Bethsaida school. The second day we buried the corpses at Sinza. We started to live with Dr. Magasha and his family and all of us were sent to schools where we lived a very happy life.

But, as for us, we thanked God. We thanked Dr. Magasha who took responsibility for us. Our father, Dr. Magasha, made us believe that NOTHING IS IMPOSSIBLE UNDER THE SUN.

Photographs of Bethsaida Girls

Classroom walk *by Lucas Ziemer*

Students work the school's vegetable garden *by Lucas Ziemer*

The Bethsaida writers clowning in the library *by Courtney Preiss*

Laughter and gardening *by Lucas Ziemer*

Morning line-up *by Lucas Ziemer*

Bethsaida Students perform at the UNSG dinner dance *by John Wakeman-Linn*

Neema at the IST computer lab

Our post editing picnic at IST school

The Bethsaida writers and and Julie Wakeman-Linn *by Courtney Preiss*

Form IV students after our second workshop *by Julie Wakeman-Linn*

Beverly Brar editing with Spora and Dorice *by Courtney Preiss*

Bethsaida writers *by Mkuki Bgoya*

A Street Girl

Prisca Emmanuel

Once upon a time there was a girl called Selestina. Both Selestina's parents died three years ago; they died of HIV/AIDS. Selestina was now an orphan when she was thirteen years old, and soon after her parents died, she stopped going to school. After the death of her parents, her uncle who called Mr. Betson decided to stay with Selestina. Mr. Betson has a wife called Anna and two children, one was called Juliette and another was called Julius. Mr. Betson was very happy when Selestina's parents died because he knew he could take all Selestina's inheritance.

One day evening Mr. Betson called Selestina and told her, "My daughter, at this time I don't have enough money to bring you to school. Now you see, if we could sell your car and house which your parents left for you, we can get money to bring you to school."

Selestina agreed with him because she liked to study and her plan was to be an accountant in the future. When Mr. Betson finished selling the things and got a lot of money, he started to change his behavior and became a drunkard and troublesome person. He drank all kinds of local beer. He drank five bottles of Gongo daily. When he was drunk, he beat his wife. Then he went to the kitchen and ate all the food. He woke up his children in the mid-night and shouted, "I'm Betson, son of Mkwawa. Who is richer than me? Wake up you puppies! Otherwise I will teach you a bad lesson!" He went on shouting and singing.

One day he went to drink as usual and he was late to come home, but Selestina was waiting for him because she was tired of his habits and a lot of disturbances. She planned to ask him about her money because she wanted to continue with her studies. When he came from drinking, he started to shout and knock at the door. "You stupid dogs come and open for the door for me."

Selestina went and opened it for him. Then he asked for food and Selestina prepared it for him.

After he finished eating, Selestina asked him in a polite language, "Father, you have promised me to send back to school when you will sell my things, but I wonder up to now there's no action you have taken apart from drinking. Is that the way of sending me back to school? I am tired of you. What kind of father are you? Give me my money. I want to continue with studies."

Mr. Betson got angry and started to shout, "To whom are you calling you Father? From today keep in your mind, I am not your father. I don't want to see you any more in my house. Go away from me, you stupid bitch! When I enter into my room, if I find you here, I will kill you."

Selestina was very afraid, and she left the house that very night. When she was walking, she met a boy.

That boy asked her, "Why are you crying? And where are you going at this mid-night?"

Selestina answered, "I don't know where I am going because my uncle chased me away and he told me he did not want to see me anymore otherwise he will kill me."

That boy started to introduce himself. "I'm Peter. How about you?"

"I'm Selestina." She looked at him through her tears. Peter looked strong enough to work and to protect her. He had a bright face and a good smile.

But Selestina was still crying. So Peter had mercy on her and decided to help her. Peter told Selestina, "Don't cry anymore, I will help you."

Selestina thanked Peter for his help and kindness. So at that midnight, Peter took Selestina to his house. When they reached home, both went to sleep.

On the next day, Peter went to steal as usual, and he left Selestina at home. When he came back home, he told Selestina, "Before you go to sleep, I want to talk to you," and Selestina agreed.

Peter approached Selestina and told her, "If you don't like me, I will chase you away from my house."

Selestina was very afraid when Peter told her that because she didn't know his background and his behavior, but she agreed with him because she had no place to go.

They started to live as husband and wife. Selestina was happy with Peter, and she did not know that Peter was a thief. And it had been two years already since Selestina and Peter met and got together. Then Selestina had a baby girl called Joa.

One day, Peter and his fellow went to steal and they found a lot of money. They decided to go somewhere so that they could celebrate their success. Suddenly, Peter met Selestina's uncle in the bar, who was already totally drunk. Peter started to ask him questions.

"Mr. Betson, what are you doing here at midnight? You have to go to bed now. Your family is waiting for you."

Mr. Betson started to provoke himself, to prepare to fight, and he told Peter that his wife has run away because of his bad behavior when he was drunk.

Mr. Betson seemed to be very desperate. At that midnight, Mr. Betson went home. When he reached home, he decided a good way to solve his situation would be to kill himself.

The next morning, a neighbor found Mr. Betson's body and soon the whole town talked about this desperate man committing suicide. When Mr. Betson's wife, Anna, heard about her husband's death, she was very happy because she knew she did not have to worry about him anymore. She thought she would help her niece but she could not find her. So Anna went back to their house with her children and lived a happier life.

One day Peter went to steal with his fellows as usual but unfortunately they were captured by police, and police decided to kill them because they were tired of them. When Selestina heard the news she got a shock and she started to cry. She was thinking, 'who is going to take care of my daughter, who is going to feed us, find us food,' while she did not have any kind of work to do and her uncle has chased her away. "I don't have a permanent house to live and I'm pregnant again." She was alone; she couldn't go to her aunt with two babies. The village would chase her away. She was then sure that her life had come to an end. She was very worried when her daughter Joa starts to cry. Selestina also cried. They were not sure of their next meal. There was no food to feed herself and her daughter. So she decided to go and sit along the roads to ask or help in order to get food and clothes. Four months later after the burial ceremony of Peter, Selestina gave birth to another daughter called Leah. These two daughters, they lost their father when they were too young, and their mother did not have any kind of work to do. She is just a beggar. This is how Selestina's life was.

A Poor Life

Angela Albert

There was a boy called Juma. When he was five years old, he joined the Iringa Boy's Primary School. His family did not have enough money to support him to join the private schools where they offer good education, so they brought him to the government school where he studied very hard. In Juma's family, they were seven -- him, his parents, two sisters and two brothers. They were not educated and they just did small activities like gardening, housekeeping, and other domestic activities in people's homes.

Due to their bad conditions they had not been even able to afford their basic needs such as food, so they had only one meal per day. Sometimes they would stay at home for a day without eating anything. Juma's father had no work to do and he just stayed in the bars, drinking alcohol. Because of their poor living conditions with no money for fees and uniforms and books, his family's poverty had caused Juma's brother to be dropped from the school. Juma studied very hard because he did not like the life he was living and he knew that education was everything and that could help him. He also knew that through education he would be able to get a very good life and help his parents and relatives. He had respect for all people at school and home as well; he was also a very hard working boy and he did what he was told to do.

Because Juma was very lovely at school, the school administration decided to help Juma regardless of his living conditions. Juma did well in all his subjects, so the school teachers were very impressed and decided to release him from school fees and to buy the books which could help him in his studies.

From that day on the school administration decided to give him support so that they could help him to reach his goals. The boy studied very hard and he was focusing towards success always. Juma used that chance very well and he got the highest marks on his exams which allowed him to reach the university.

When he completed his studies; he was employed by the university as a lecturer. Due to that position, he got money and started to help his village by educating them on how to open small businesses, like dukas to sell fruits and vegetables. He also taught the children in his village subjects like mathematics and English. These students performed well. The villagers were so proud to get such a good education. So all the people in the village worked very hard, and also the children studied very hard. After a few years passed, all the families had a good life, and escaped from poverty.

Also Juma's family became improved because of Juma. He helped his relatives by opening for them small businesses like a shoe repair shop, and he bought for them a taxi and a bajaji to give them business activities. So, at the end, Juma succeeded in his goal and everyone who knew him realized that 'where there is a will, there is a way.'

John and Rehema

Beatrice Karol

Once upon the time there was a certain family living in Dar-es-Salaam. In that family there lived a father, mother and two children. The first born was known as John and the last born was called Rehema. John and Rehema were enjoying life with Father and Mother. Their parents were earning a lot of money which helped them to get food, education, shelter and clothes. They lived in peace, respecting one another. John and Rehema were studying in a school known as Mwenge Primary School. When John was in standard three, his young sister was in standard one. They were studying hard so that they could perform well.

One day their father and mother were traveling from Dar-es-Salaam to Kilimanjaro to greet their parents. Suddenly when they reached Mombo, they were in an accident. All the people who were on that bus died. Thus they did not succeed in reaching Kilimanjaro.

The accident happened on Monday at 10.00 am at Mombo. The policeman decided to bring all corpses to the mortuary in Mombo. Meanwhile, John and Rehema at home were thinking, 'which day will Father and Mother come back home? Then the next day, which was Tuesday, during nighttime, the police announced on television what happened to the bus from Dar-es-salaam to Kilimanjaro. Rehema and John were watching TV and heard the announcement about the accident. Both of them started to cry and did not know what to do. They cried because they knew that their parents had died and they wouldn't see them again.

The next day all neighbors had a meeting so that they could help the children to take bodies of their parents from Mombo Mortuary to Dar es Salaam. The burial ceremony was on Friday and all neighbors were sad.

Two weeks after the burial ceremony the children went to their grandmother in Kilimanjaro and started a new life. Six months passed and the grandmother did not have enough money to provide basic needs for them like clothes, shelter and food. That condition led them to become street children begging for food and when people refused to give them anything, they were stealing.

When they were begging for the food and money, some people were giving the food which was only ugali and beans. The money which they gave was only one hundred shillings, two hundred schillings, only small coins which was not enough to buy food. Other children were laughing at them and beating them. Rehema and John felt bad.

They were not going to school because their grandmother had no money. But the grandmother was thinking every day how could she help the children so that they could get food, shelter, and education.

Their uncle, who lived in Kigoma did not often go to see his mother. One day he was talking by telephone to his friend who was living in Kilimanjaro and was told that his mother was living in bad conditions.

The next day he decided to travel from Kigoma to Kilimanjaro so that he could greet his mother and friends. When he reached his mother's home he found Rehema, John and his mother living a very poor life. That condition made him feel sad and he decided to help his mother and those children by giving them enough food, shelter and clothes. He brought Rehema and John to school. So from that day Rehema and John were very happy to go back to school. Also their grandmother was very happy. Most of the other children who had been laughing at them became their friends again. Of course they missed their parents and sometime they felt very sad about what had happened in their life. But now their life is not too bad.

Vaileth's Story

Josina Jason

Vaileth was an orphan girl living with her uncle and aunt. Her parents died a longtime ago when Vaileth was very young. Her mother died soon after bearing Vaileth and her father died a few years later so she lived with her uncle and aunt who were staying in Mwanza and they had children whom Vaileth called cousins. Her Aunt was called Cecilia and she was very educated and loving to people. Cecilia also loved Vaileth in such a way that one day when Vaileth remembered her parents and started to cry, Cecilia also was very sad thinking about what was wrong with Vaileth.

"What is wrong with you, girl? You have been crying so much?" asked Cecilia.

"Nothing is wrong, Aunt," said Vaileth, "I miss my parents."

"I miss my sister, your mother, too. That's why I want to try to go abroad to study to so women do not die from bleeding too much like your mother did, " Cecilia said. "It will be wonderful to become a specialist doctor."

Vaileth thought about being a specialist doctor when she was grown up and she also desired to help women and poor people and widows and orphans when she got some money. Vaileth was also thinking about the family she would have when she was grown up and hoped to have a very handsome husband with three children.

Vaileth grew up together with her cousins who shared their time with her in sports, gardening, and telling different stories. When it reached time for Vaileth to go to school, her uncle did not take her to school. Instead he took only his children to school and Vaileth was told to stay at home and do all the housework which was supposed to be done, such as washing clothes and dishes, sweeping, cooking and cleaning the environment, while she was still so young.

Her uncle started humiliating and abusing her by requiring hard work which she did without any payment. One day her aunt got a scholarship to go outside the county for her professional studies and Vaileth remained at home with her uncle because her cousins also were away at the boarding school. Because her aunt was not around, her uncle raped Vaileth and warned her not to tell anyone, even her aunt when she came back from her studies. Vaileth kept on being forced by her uncle who was a very stubborn, cruel drunkard.

After few months had passed she got pregnant, and when she informed her uncle about it, he started complaining and he denied the pregnancy. He also told people that Vaileth had bad behavior of playing with boys, and when she went to market, she was late to come home. He claimed that was how she got pregnant.

"I'm tired of this girl," the uncle said.

"Why are you talking like this about Vaileth?" asked the villagers.

"This is too much. Now she is playing around with boys," he said.

The whole village blamed her in such a way that she was confused and drank some poison which caused the miscarriage of her pregnancy and her uncle chased her away. She became crazy due to the problems she faced which made her do dangerous things like walking on the road when the cars were speeding by and also staying in dangerous areas like the rubbish dump which had smoking trash. Her lungs were destroyed by the smoke and caused her to suffer from TB. She also ate the foods which had spoiled, and due to that, she suffered from cholera and because she had no help, she died.

When her aunt Ceceilia came from abroad and found Vaileth had died, she did not believe what her husband said to her because she knew Vaileth couldn't do such things. So she decided to leave her husband. She told the family what happened which made Vaileth's uncle ashamed and he ran away from the village. So the aunt got a job and finally she was one of the best specialist doctors in the country and she was employed at Muhimbili hospital helping women. She lived happily without a husband and managed to take care of her children.

Hope in Tears

Spora Gibron

On a certain day when Charity was in Botswana for her studies, she made a friend whose name was Comfort. They lived together in one house which Comfort's family had bought for them because, even though Comfort's parents were living in Botswana, they lived so far away from the school. The girls loved each other. They usually awakened early in morning to prepare themselves for school. But Saturdays and Sundays they used to sleep longer and wake up late. It was hard for them because they had so many studies and at home they had to do all the housework and cook their meals so they got very tired. Comfort's parents had mercy on them and they found a maid to work for them.

When they were at home one Friday evening, Charity went out in the garden. She lifted her eyes to the sky where she saw that the stars and moon were bright. There was a big shooting star, surrounded by brightly glinting small stars like a small birds of different colours playing around a river.

She was very surprised, so she called her friend Comfort and said to her, "I want to surprise you."

"Do you?" her friend asked. Charity pointed to the stars. Before saying anything they looked at each other with love and happiness and then they looked together at the sky for a while. They saw the moon and the stars flashing.

Comfort looked at Charity and said, "This is a wonderful day to be remembered all our lives. What do you think?"

Charity replied, "Sure, it really is," so they went into their room and brought a camera to take the photos of the sky and each other as a memory.

Their servant, whose name was Faith, started to call them in to sleep because they had stayed out to 1 a.m., but when nobody replied she went out to follow them. Once she saw what made Charity and Comfort to stay out for such a time, she was also amazed with the sky and joined them. They kept watching until they fell asleep.

Three months later Charity got the information that her parents had died in an air crash coming from Ghana, which was their mother country, on their way to visit Charity at school in Botswana. So Charity had to go back to her country to attend her parents' funeral. After her parents' funeral ceremony ended, Charity's relatives took all the inheritance of Charity's parents. Charity remained with nothing. She had no way to return to school and they decided that she would stay at her relatives' house and work for them as a maid. Although she stayed home as a maid for a long time, she still wanted to go to school and she always remembered the time she spent at school with her friend, Comfort, in Botswana. When she remembered her friend she used to look up to the peaceful sky which made her feel close to Comfort. This made her happy.

Back in Botswana, her friend, Comfort, was completing her studies. She worried about Charity every day. After two years, when she was graduating, she told her father she felt sad to be without her friend. Her father asked about Charity, and she told her father that Charity was in her own country and didn't have anyone to help her to continue with her studies.

Comfort's parents were not happy about that news. They suggested finding any means to communicate with Charity in order to help her go to school. Comfort's parents sent a ticket to Charity from Ghana to Botswana. Once she got the ticket, tears fell down because of joy. She asked for permission from her uncle and aunt, but they talked to her in bad ways and insulted her. This is because they didn't want Charity to have a good life. They were very jealous hearing that she wanted to go back in Botswana for school and they didn't allow her to go. Bad enough, they were very cruel and stubborn to her which made her to escape to Botswana. When she reached Botswana, she met with her best friend who had already left her behind in studies for two years. Of course she was not happy because they had planned to finish together and their dream had been broken.

Charity was brought to school by Comfort's parents and she succeeded in her studies to go university where she became close again with Comfort. After their studies Comfort became a doctor and Charity was a lawyer who fought and got her wealth back which her parents had left her.

Now Charity is helpful in the world and who loved by everyone. She helps the orphans, old people, patients and all who need help. Both Charity and Comfort still are friends and famous in the whole of Botswana.

They celebrated their friendship and the memory of the night sky with a big party at an international hotel in Tanzania. The hotel was built on the ocean surrounded by water, with a good garden which had hibiscus and gardenia flowers. They invited many people to their party, and actually it was really good. The MC asked Charity and Comfort to stay in the garden which was prepared especially for them. They looked like African Queens. The girls embraced each other with big smiles and all the people in the party stood up and clapped for them in the shining light from the big moon and twinkling stars.

A FRIEND'S EFFORT MADE SOMEONE'S DREAMS COME TRUE

My Friend, Terry

Eusebia Mrema

The name of my best friend is Terry, and when she was nineteen years old, she was in form six. Terry and I were in the same class. She was a slim but smart girl. She was not only intelligent but also a hardworking girl. She always stood first or second in the class. She was good at English and Kiswahili; she became a favorite student of all the teachers.

Her house was not very far from mine, so after school hours I would go to her house and we would do our homework together. Although Terry knew science subjects better than arts, she would help me in doing arts homework whenever I had any difficulties. Because she was their first child, her parents Mr. Kelly and Mrs. Dorothy were much interested in her studies. So they provided her with all requirements, like books, clothes, and shoes. They believed that if she studied well, all her young brothers and sisters would follow her. They always advised her to respect her teachers. They believed in hard work because it never goes unrewarded. So many times they advised us to do hard work. Their intention was to make her a doctor. After finishing her studies, she passed her exams and I did too, and we continued with our studies at University of Dar es Salaam.

Once we were there she got a boyfriend named Jonathan, a playboy who liked many girls. I always advised her to be wary of boys until she finished up her studies because boys always destroy girls' lives. But she was blind and she did not stop loving him. Terry began to have many challenges. She joined a bad group of friends who always told her to go to the party instead of studying. She started to fail her exams. Her habits started to change which made her parents worried about her. She even refused to study because of Jonathan.

One day Terry went to a club with Jonathan and that day she did not come to class. I was unhappy because I didn't see her in the class.

After class I decided to go to her home to ask for her, and her parents told me that since morning they hadn't seen her.

She had gone to the party with her friends, and when they were at the party Jonathan met another girl called Natasha. Jonathan left Terry alone and started to follow Natasha. So Terry started to quarrel with Jonathan by insulting him. Jonathan insulted her too, and started to beat her. Terry was screaming and making noise. Jonathan beat Terry until she became unconscious, which made everybody worry. Quickly people brought her to the hospital and Jonathan was caught by a policeman. Her parents were informed of the bad news about Terry. They went to the hospital where Terry was and found her covered with wounds all over her body. They had mercy on her because she couldn't talk, even to explain what happened.

The next morning when I was at school I heard people talking about what happened to Terry. I was shocked and thought a lot about her and I decided to go and visit her in the hospital. When I reached there I found Terry's parents. When I looked at Terry, I started to cry and Terry was crying too, because she remembered my advice that boys are dangerous, but she had refused to listen to me.

Later on she recovered enough to continue with her studies. She promised her parents that she would study hard. But when she came back to university and found me, it was my last year at university. She was very sad because I was going to leave her alone, but I kept on advising her to study hard so that she could fulfill her dreams. When the time of my exams came I did well and when the results came out I performed well and later became a professor. Soon Terry phoned and congratulated me.

After three years, when I was at my office, I got a call from Terry and she told me that she was going to do her exams. After one month the result was out and she had performed well. She was selected to join to a medical college at the University of Dar es Salaam. There, she studied hard, and due to her efforts of studying very hard, she became a gynecologist who deals with human disease. Her parents decided to congratulate her with a big party and she invited me to be a guest of honor at the party. From that day we lived happy lives.

Fighting for Freedom

Neema Patrick Tarimo

My name is Alice. My mother's name is Lisa and my father' name is Francis. I was born in 1946 in Tasmonia. Both my mother and father were descended from slaves. They were treated badly because they were black. My mother's family was from Zimbabwe and my father's family was from Tanzania.

We were living in a poor life because it was very hard for a black person to be employed. Black people were not allowed to work with whites. If they were found out, they were punished. I didn't like the condition. I wished I could change it.

When I reached the age of five years, I was sent to school. The school had both black and whites but there were different classes; some were for whites and others which were for blacks. I was not happy with the condition. I had a dream to change it. There were buses when we came from school but black people were not allowed to sit. No black person could sit while a white person had no place to sit.

There were different places where you could not find a black person and there were other places where you could not find a white person. Black people were drinking water in the water fountains which were labeled "coloured." I did not like it at all. I wanted to study very hard so I could change it.

I wanted to save my fellow blacks. I wanted to fight for our rights and that was my secret. I didn't tell it to anyone, even my parents who I loved very much.

When I was seven years old, I had a white friend, Molly. I loved her very much and she loved me too. One day as we were going together to school, her father saw her with me. He wondered very much at what he saw and he asked his daughter why was she walking with me.

His daughter told him that I was her best friend , but her father told her that she was not allowed to walk with a black person. She asked him "why" but he did not talk to her again, instead he was talking to me. "Whenever I see you with my daughter I will cut off your head, you black dog." I had nothing more to say other than crying. I left my friend Molly crying also and I ran back home. I was very sad. My parents were also very sad when I told them the story. My mother cried.

The next day I saw her but I didn't want to follow her. She wanted to follow me, but I told her not to follow me.

Life in Tasmonia was tough but I studied very hard until I reached university. In the university things were different because we used the same classes with whites but there were only a few black students who had reached universities. Chairs and tables used by blacks were different from those used by whites. Whites had their own dining halls and blacks had their own dining halls. Still we blacks were drinking water in the fountains labeled "colored." It was terrible.

I choose my friend a girl who was black as I was and she was called Gloria. She was originally from Nigeria. Both her father and mother were taken as slaves from Nigeria. I was very happy to be with her. I told her every thing about me because I trusted her very much. I even told her my secret that I wanted to fight for black people's rights and she also told me that she had that kind of wish too. I was very happy because I now had a friend who would help me in making my dreams come true.

When we finished our university studies, we started our work. It was very hard to travel all over Tasmonia because people were not paying attention to our message, but we didn't give up. We discussed together what to do so people would pay attention to us. We called for a black people's meeting in our own conference hall. We told them that it was the time for us to fight for our rights.

"We have to find out a solution. We should be given the same rights as whites. Why should whites discriminate against us? What have we done?" I asked them and they answered together, "Nothing."

We told them how good it will be if we will have our rights that we will get enough employment and we will not be poor any more.

Gloria and I were always cooperating together, although our fellow black people were not giving us cooperation at first, but at least now they were trying to show a spirit that they wanted their freedom.

We reached the time period that white soldiers were arresting us and giving us beatings, but still we had to fight because we knew that "never is there a Rose without thorns." So we didn't give up. When my friend Gloria was tired, I was telling her to rest. Then I was going alone and announced "We black people, We are not animals. We should not be treated like wild dogs. We want our freedom."

We printed posters and wrote "Black people are tired. They are crying for their freedom." We passed all over Tasmonia and distributed them. We gave them to the government which made the president become very harsh to us, so that he sent the soldiers to arrest and jail us. Still we did not give up. We prayed to God because we knew that God was everything to us. And because of our prayers to God, the government was about to hear our crying. The President called for a meeting with his government. Finally they agreed to give black people freedom. They accepted our call to stop whites from feeling superior to blacks.

This was a very beautiful day that we had a meeting of all the people in Tasmonia. It was in 1963 when the government gathered all the people and the president announced freedom for black people.

I was with my friend and we sat together with both my parents and her parents and we were very happy. My mother was so very happy that she was always hugging me.

We carefully listened to the president. "We have given you freedom because of the efforts made by two ladies who were always ready to come and ask for your freedom. These ladies were Alice Francis and Gloria Samwel."

Many black people came to say thanks to us for saving their lives. We were very happy. Everyone cheered.

There was a general election in which some black people were elected to join the government with whites. Gloria and I were also elected. I was elected to be a Minister of Social Matters and Gloria became a Commissioner of International Political Matters. We were very happy. Many black people were happy with the election.

And soon after the election we were known all over the world through telecommunication broadcasts. Everyone wanted to see us personally and give us presents. We got a lot of presents that day..

After all announcements about election, Gloria came close to me and then we hugged each other happily. Then we prayed and thanked God together. We thanked God for his love and care that he gave us when we were fighting for freedom.

I looked at her and she looked at me, then we told each other, "Be blessed forever."

We sang together a beautiful friendship song saying "We will be friends forever."

Contributors Notes

My name is Neema Patrick Tarimo. I'm 17 years old. I was born in Tanzania in the region called Kilimanjaro. I like reading history novels. In my future I want to become a linguistic. I like writing stories, especially history stories, because that is my favorite subject. I love music and speaking English. I hate discrimination and I promise I will fight against any kind of discrimination, like discrimination against women in Tanzania and most of Africa. I want to write another story that will be titled, "Fighting for Women's Freedom." So wait to get it from me soon!

My name is Dorice Kessy. I am from Kilimanjaro. My favorite subjects are history, geography, and civics. I would like to be a lawyer or a journalist. I like singing and listening to all kinds of music. My best teacher was Jerry Ndalenga. I love my school, Bethsaida, because it is not only a secondary school but also a life building school where morals and goals are developed. I like chocolat, and I love my friend Jenn, and all the people who help special groups , like orphans, who can't afford basic necessities such as food, shelter and clothes.

My name is Dorice Peter. I come from Mbeya. My favorite subjects are history and English. I would like to be a lawyer. I like to play netball. I love my family very much. I am the first born in my family. When I grow up, I want to help orphans. I like to worship the Lord and thank him for giving me good health.

My name is Jackline Njawa. I come from Ruvuma. My favorite subjects history, geography. I want to be a lawyer. I like dance music and visiting my relatives. In my free time, I prefer to communicate with people through phone. My favorite sport is football. I like bananas. My best teacher was Jerry Ndalang.

My name is Prisca Emmanuel. I come from Kilimanjaro. My favorite subjects are math, physics, geography and languages. I want to be an accountant. I like English songs. My favorite food is rice and bananas. I like chatting with friends. In my free time, I like reading novels and computer research. When I will have my own work, I would like to help people like orphans and street children, and people who are in need.

My name is Josina Jason. I am from Kagera. My favorite subjects are English, Biology, and geography. I would like to be a doctor. I enjoy R&B music and chatting with friends. When I get money, I would like to support poor people. My grateful thanks go to those who support me, most especially my school, Bethsaida.

My name is Eusebia Mrema, and I come from Kilimanjaro. My favorite subjects are biology, physics, and chemistry. I would like to be a doctor. I like my school, Bethsaida, and all the people who support my school, especially the UN groups. May the Lord bless them. I love sharing different ideas with my friend. I love all the people around me. I speak two languages, English and Kiswahili. I like praying and studying.

My name is Angela Albert. I come from Dodoma. I like geography, math, history and language. I want to be an accountant. I like writing different stories, because it is part of increasing my knowledge and ideas. In my free time I prefer to visit sick people in hospital, and given them hope where it is needed.

My names is Anna Joseph. I come from the coastal region in Tanzania. My best subjects are history and Kiswahili and English. I want to be a lawyer. I like to pray and to play. In my life, I want to help people who need help. I like my friends, and enjoy listening to music and dancing. I like my family very much, and also my best friends and those who help me in my life.

My name is Beatrice Karol. I come from Kilimanjaro. In the future I want to be an accountant. I like to study geography and mathematics. I like to run, and I like singing gospel songs. In the future, I would like to help people who are suffering, like orphans, street children, and people suffering from HIV/AIDS. I like to encourage people who are in a bad condition, and to share ideas with them. I love all people.

My name is Cecilia Mwanayongo. I come from Sumbawanga in Tanzania. I like to study physics and I would like to be an Engineer. I like to advise people and to encourage them. I love and respect all people. I like singing, and I am a good singer. In my free time, I like ot worship the Lord and thank him for the wonderful life he gives me always. I love my sisters, and all orphans in the world.

My name is Spora Gibron. I come from Arusha in Tanzania. I like to study biology, geography and English, and I would like to be a biologist. I like to make people happy. I like to sing, to listen to songs, swimming, and making things. For example, I like making cards of different shapes.

My name is Chiku Shabani, and I am from Tabora. My favorite subjects are history, English, and Kiswahili. My favorite teacher at Bethsaida was Maristella. I like my guardians, Hamissa and Hamisi, very much. I want to be a judge. When I get my own work, I would like to help street children and orphans.

Julie Wakeman-Linn is on leave from Montgomery College, Rockville, Maryland where she teaches English composition and creative writing. Her short stories have appeared in *Rosebud, Santa Clara Review, Grey Sparrow Review*, and several other literary magazines. Her novel, *Chasing the Leopard*, was a finalist for Barbara Kingsolver's Bellwether Prize. She edited the *Potomac Review* until December 2010.

Lucas Ziemer: After finishing high school I decided to go from my nice hometown Leipzig in Germany abroad to do a one year social service instead of the military service. This is how I came to Bethsaida (Dar es Salaam, Tanzania) and was able to experience a wonderful year with a lot of things I have learned aboud culture, people and live. It was also a nice chance to go on with my big hobby of taking pictures and I am very glad about getting the chance of showing them because as Dorothea Lange once wrote "a camera is a instrument which teaches people to see without the camera". In the future I want to be a doctor and go on with working with people and connect it with my hobby.